Broke

Act One
Part Eight

Chris Wooding

Cover and illustrations by Steve Kyte

SCHOLASTIC

Scholastic Children's Books,
Commonwealth House, 1-19 New Oxford Street,
London WC1A 1NU, UK
a division of Scholastic Ltd
London ~ New York ~ Toronto ~ Sydney ~ Auckland
Mexico City ~ New Delhi ~ Hong Kong

First published in the UK by Scholastic Ltd, 1999

Text copyright © Chris Wooding, 1999
Illustrations copyright © Steve Kyte, 1999

ISBN 0 439 01100 0

Typeset by M Rules
Printed by Cox and Wyman Ltd, Reading, Berks.

10 9 8 7 6 5 4 3 2 1

Other books by Chris Wooding:
Crashing
Point Horror Unleashed: Catchman
Kerosene

www.homestead.gar_jenna

Broken Sky

TY

KETTIN

THE BEAR CLAW

1

Loose of Their Cages

"Sit down, please," Ty offered, and she did.

His quarters were a spartan affair, a round room at the top of a short, stumpy two-storey tower of hastily-laid bricks and wood. There was little in it but a sleeping pallet, a stone washbasin and a wide, jagged piece of polished metal that was used as a mirror. There was also a narrow fireplace, in which embers still smouldered, and a roughly-carved chair before it. The ceiling was high, the rafters disappearing in the darkness above; the floorboards creaked underfoot.

But none of this interested Kia as she sat down on the edge of the pallet. She was watching only Ty, as he crouched with his back to her, stirring up the fire and feeding it fresh fuel. His appearance had changed so much. His unkempt, wild black hair was gone. His narrow shoulders and bare arms were now corded with lean muscle. He no longer wore simple stable garments, but hardwearing boots and a motley assortment of whatever he had been able to scavenge together to clothe himself.

He finished stoking the fire and drew the chair up in front of her, then sat down, too. For a long while, they just looked at each other; she with her dirtied and beautiful face under a tangle of red hair, he with his drastically new appearance, one side red and one side blue. Finally, it was Ty who spoke.

"You came to find me?" he said, his voice not as strong as he might have liked.

Kia smiled, her eyes still raw from the long-overdue tears she had shed. "Yeah," she said.

"Thanks."

"S'okay."

A pause. They both looked at their knees awkwardly.

"It's good to see you," she said at last.

"I'm glad . . . you got out. Of Osaka Stud."

"I thought you were dead," she replied.

"I know. So did I," he smiled weakly. "The stables collapsed after they blew out the hub. But I was right on the rim, in the lock-chamber. They built it pretty sturdily, I guess. But still, most of it fell down on me." He looked into the greenness of her irises. "They dug me out. Some of their Guardsmen were trapped inside, and they found me by accident. They figured I wasn't dead yet, so they put me with the captives. That's how I got here."

"Oh Ty, I'm *sorry*," Kia blurted. "We left you. We left you behind."

He took her hands in his, touching her as he had never dared do before. "Hey, it's okay. Why do you think I lied to you about where Banto was? I knew you'd never leave otherwise. *I'm* sorry. I'm sorry I had to deceive you."

"I knew you lied," she said, her voice quiet. "I think, even then, I knew you were lying."

She hung her head, reeling under the barrage of

emotions that had seeped through the chinks in her armour at the sight of him. It was Ty's voice that she heard – it was so *good* to hear – but it was infused with a new confidence, a new strength now. No longer was he the shy, unsure boy that she had left behind; and yet he *was*, still, tender and sweet and sensitive underneath.

She shuddered, flinching under the sudden rush of an emotion she did not recognize. She pulled her hands away from his, and was strangely gratified to see him drop them hastily, as if he thought he'd gone too far, overstepped his boundaries.

"What happened?" she asked, more out of the need to say something than the need to know anything specific. She let him make up his own mind what she meant.

"They questioned me," he said, leaning back, his face disappearing into shadow. "I told them what I knew. Then they . . . questioned me some more."

"What did you know?" Kia asked.

"Nothing," he replied. "Did you?"

"I didn't then. I do now," she replied.

"So do I," he answered, letting his voice trail off. Then he seemed to come back to himself. "Anyway, when they were done, they took me to Os Dakar. I think they were going to execute me, because you and me had been. . ." He paused, then finished: "Friends." He looked at her, his eyes nervously roaming her features. "But at the last minute, an order came through. I was told it was from Macaan himself. So they didn't kill me. They sent me here instead."

"You seem like a hero here," Kia ventured. "With the Bear Claw, surely the tribe need you more than—"

"I'm a *killer* here!" he snapped, suddenly standing up, his chair falling over behind him. Kia's eyes mirrored her shock. He turned away, unable to bear the wounded look there, and walked to stand in front of the fire, silhouetted against the light.

"I'm sorry," he said at last. "At times, I almost get used to it. I accept it, y'know? I mean, I've been here long enough to pick up the lingo, the crazy speech they talk, but. . ." He hunkered down in front of the fire. "Here I'm accepted. Here they need me. They like me. They have respect for me. More than they ever would for someone who's only been here a few months. Sometimes I think

I'm one of them." He turned round, and his eyes were a dark glimmer in his painted face. "And then something happens, like you, and I remember what I used to be, and what I've become."

"What *have* you become?" Kia asked.

"A murderer," he replied. "I live, I earn my place in this tribe, by driving the Bear Claw. Kia, if you could *see* what it *does* to people. . ." His shoulders sagged. "You shouldn't have come for me," he said. "I'm not what you remember."

"You *are* what I remember," she said, getting to her feet and pacing restlessly. "You think you're the only one who's been changed by this? I have . . . *such* a *hate* inside me. A hatred for Macaan, for the Guardsmen, for everything and everyone that killed my father. I let it go in Tusami City. In a crowded market. Cetra knows how many innocents I might have killed, if it had gone another way." She stopped, her hands gripping the side of her hair. "But I killed those Guardsmen. I've done that much. And if you're a murderer, that makes me a murderer, too."

"You're not a murderer," Ty said, quietly insistent. "Not you. It was self-defence."

"It *wasn't* self-defence, Ty," Kia replied stridently. "It was *war*. I didn't ask to be part of it, and neither did you. But both of us have had to kill to stay alive. That's the game Macaan has brought us into. And if either of us hadn't done what we had to, I wouldn't be standing here and you wouldn't have lasted two days in this place."

She let the weight of her words settle in the silence that followed them. Then she spoke again, her voice softer.

"Ty, we didn't want to be made into what we are. We both want things to be like they were before. But that's gone now, all of it. We have to go on."

Another long silence, broken only by the snapping of the growing fire. When next Ty spoke, he changed the subject entirely, not wishing to think about what she had said.

"We found your friends, too."

Kia swivelled urgently. "You'd better not have put *them* through what me and Gerdi—"

"No, it's okay," he said. "Whist told us where he had left the rest of the newcomers; that was as much as I knew when I went along. I recognized Elani and Ryushi when we got there. I told the party that had been sent to capture them that they were friends of mine. I talked to Elani. She told me where you'd gone, and I came right back. A little late, I guess."

"I'm still here," she said.

"They put all the newcomers in the Snapper Run," he said apologetically. "Whist keeps an eye out for fresh arrivals, and brings them to Kettin, the tribal captain. If they beat the Snapper Run, they're allowed to join the tribe."

"What if they don't want to?" Kia asked.

"Nobody says no," Ty replied. "Look around you, Kia. You think you'd survive here on your own? Even Whist, for all his talking about being independent, has to rely on us to some extent."

"But why all the charade? Why go to all the trouble of breaking in?"

"It's Whist's thing," Ty said. "He has to prove to himself that he can get in and out whenever he wants. Kettin humours him and turns a blind eye to it. He's good, though. He always manages to lead people to us without a fight."

"Yeah, I noticed," said Kia, remembering the trap he had sprung on her. "So where are the others, anyway?"

"They're in quarters. They're my guests. Kettin gives me a lot of privileges like that, in return for . . . what I do for him. That's how I got those Damper Collars taken off you and Gerdi, to start with."

"Can I see them? Ryushi and the others."

"We have to talk first," Ty replied. It wasn't really a request. The old Ty would never have spoken like that; but then, the old Ty, like a lot of things, had changed. He got up from the fire and walked over to her, so that they stood face-to-face in the growing warmth of the room. "Kia, listen. This is important. They took me places, when they were questioning me. I saw and heard things, things I didn't really understand then, but now I do."

"I don't—"

"*Listen*," he hissed, and then, gentler: "Please, Kia. This might be the only chance I get to tell you this, and someone has to know. A lot of people come to Os Dakar, from the Dominions and from Kirin Taq. A lot of people, from a lot of places, who've seen things like I have. Maybe it's only because we're all gathered here, that only we seem to be able to see the whole picture. But we're the only people who can't do anything *about* it."

He turned away, walked over to the fire and

stared into it once again, as if, within its flames, he could find the words he needed.

"Do you have a way to get out of here?" he asked.

"Yeah," she replied.

"Then promise me that, whatever happens to me, you'll get away to get this information to the people who can use it."

"No."

His shaven head half-turned, paused. "No?"

"I've left too many people behind," she said. "I've lost too many. I'm not doing it again, Ty. It hurts too much." She walked over and stood next to him, staring into the heart of the fire as he did. "I promise you that I'm not leaving Os Dakar without you, and that's the only way I *am* going. That's the best you'll get from me."

She expected an argument from him, but he gave her none. "You always did know your own mind," he said, his voice curving into a smile.

"I did," she said. "I'd like to again, one day."

Her words seemed to fall dead as they came from her mouth. The fire crackled noisily. The rafters above them were half-seen cross-beams spanning a pit of shadow.

"After Macaan had ordered me taken to Os Dakar," Ty said, "they took me to a Ley Warren. That's what they called it. It's like . . . it's like that one time, when we went out really far from the Stud, and there was that valley. You remember?"

"I remember."

"And when we were there, we saw that termite colony? Those big towers of solid earth, taller than

15

we were, six or seven of them of different heights and shapes, all linked together? We called it the City of the Termites, remember? And we couldn't believe that things so small could make something so huge."

"Yeah," said Kia, with a smile. How strange, that she had been thinking of exactly the same event when she had formulated the plan to get into Os Dakar. "It seems a long time ago."

"This Ley Warren," he continued. "That was what it was like. Except it was as if *I* was the termite, the *size* of an termite in comparison. And inside it, everywhere . . . Keriags. Thousands upon thousands of them. They're hiding them in there. The Guardsmen on the outside keep people out, while the Keriags build from the inside up."

Kia felt a rill of repulsion run across her face as she thought of the black, shiny skins of the insectile Keriags.

"I don't know how many of those things work under Macaan, but I know there are at least seven of those Ley Warrens, from what people here have told me. They're all over the Dominions. But that's not all. They're all over Kirin Taq as well."

Something that Calica had said before they left Gar Jenna, relayed to her by Ryushi during the few times they had spoken, blinked across Kia's mind: it had been to do with strange constructions that had recently appeared at certain regions in the Dominions.

"What are they?" she asked.

"I don't know," he replied. "I was taken there to meet a Resonant; I think it was one Macaan had

17

newly captured. He took me over to Kirin Taq, so I could be transported to Os Dakar."

Kia frowned. "But why would he send you here?" she mused to herself.

"That's not everything," Ty continued. "Kettin, the leader of the Fallen Sun . . . his brother was a Resonant. He was one of the first to be taken when Macaan started rounding them up."

"To the Ley Warrens?" Kia asked. "Is *that* where they're being taken?"

Ty nodded, his newly-unfamiliar face washed by the firelight. "Kettin followed them, and led a group in to try and get his brother out. He was one of the best thieves there was. King Macaan himself was staying there, in temporary quarters, overseeing . . . whatever it was they were doing. Kettin went in there to get his brother, but he couldn't resist the chance of seeing what he could get from the King's quarters." He smiled faintly. "I guess he's always been a thief at heart. Anyway, Kettin was captured, along with the rest of them; but not before he'd stolen King Macaan's own earring from where it lay on his dressing-table. He says that, if Macaan had been there, he could've killed him and been done with it all." Ty paused. "He never found his brother. He was sent to Os Dakar. He managed to hide the earring by swallowing it. He wears it still."

But Kia jerked around at his words, sudden realization on her face. She grabbed him by the shoulders. In the polished-metal mirror above the washbasin, reflected figures moved in synchronicity.

"Macaan's *earring*? And it is really his? Ty, if we could get that, we could find out *everything*!"

"What? How?"

Kia tried to calm her mounting excitement, but she was still speaking breathlessly. "Calica, back at Gar Jenna. She's psychometric. She can tell the past from touching an object. That earring might have been worn by Macaan all the time he was planning this. If we can get it to her . . . we'll know everything!"

"Are you sure?"

"It's a chance!"

"He'll never part with it."

"Then we'll take it off him!"

Now it was Ty's turn to grip her shoulders, steadying her firmly. His eyes, once so soft, now bored into her.

"Kia, stop."

She stopped, chastened. Having kept her emotions under such strict rein for so long, she was embarrassed to find them raging uncontrollably within her, like long-penned beasts that had broken loose of their cages. When she had quieted, her face tilted expectantly, he spoke.

"I can't leave this place," he said, and then raised a hand to hush her as she drew breath to protest. "They'll never let me go. The Fallen Sun were just another tribe until Whist found me. They'd been waiting for a Pilot for months. The Bear Claw was already built. But now, with me, they're the strongest. They can rule this island. They can make it safe, regulate it, turn Os Dakar from a war-zone into one big tribe. It's Kettin's dream: to make Os Dakar whole. We can do it in secret; nobody ever checks what goes on here. Once we all work together, neither Macaan nor Princess Aurin can hold us in."

"You sound like you agree with him," Kia said flatly.

"I agree with the principle. Not the method."

"Because you're still a murderer. In your own eyes."

Ty released her, as if unwilling to touch her after she had dealt him such a cruel reminder. It seemed her ability to wound had not entirely deserted her upon finding Ty at last.

"It is a foolish man who rages against what he cannot change," he said quietly.

"Muachi, right? The philosopher?"

"Right."

"You remember the day Father died, you told

me about The Game? That was Muachi, too. The Game of Man and Woman."

"You said that you didn't know it," Ty replied, recalling it as if it was yesterday. "I said you wouldn't play by the rules if you did."

"That's right, I wouldn't play by the rules," she said. "But I never said I wouldn't *play*."

And with those words, the final barriers between them collapsed, the fear that each of them held of allowing another to care for them, and they met in a kiss that had the force of years behind it, as if it had long been destined to happen but had only now been allowed to. They kissed each other desperately, dissolving into one another, and Ty knew that he could not live without Kia now, and she knew that she would risk anything to take him with her from this place, and

23

tears fell from both of them as, finally, their scarred souls began to heal.

From where he hid in the rafters, Whist watched, digesting all that he had heard, arranging it for Kettin's ears.

From behind the polished-metal mirror, unseen by the two figures entwined before the fire or the one that hid in the shadows, a telescopic brass eyepiece whirred, focusing.

2

Much Prey Tonight

"Goodgreet, tribe-brother Ty," said Mila, her weathered face creasing into a smile as she saw him. Once, she had been pretty, a Harvest Queen of a small Dominion village. Then she had fallen for the wrong man, a traitor to the King. When he had been caught and executed, she had been implicated and imprisoned. Her time on Os Dakar had ravaged her beauty with strife and battle, and buried it under the painted halves of the Fallen

Sun's tribal colours. The sheen of her silver-blue hair had faded; but when she smiled, a glimmer of what had once been showed through.

"Goodgreet, Mila," Ty replied. "Is tribe-captain Kettin inside, nai?"

They were standing outside Kettin's quarters, a three-storey building with the lowest floor made of stone and the upper two constructed of lighter wood. A balcony jutted out above them, overhanging; a sentry stood at each corner, watching the surrounding camp. Nothing could get close without being seen.

But Ty was known here, and he wore the tribal colours, and so he had walked under the unwavering gaze of the sentries and up to the door – a thick wooden affair that hung slightly off-angle due to poor workmanship on the hinges – and up to Mila, Kettin's door-sentry ever since Ty arrived, and long before. Torches rippled flame in their brackets, lightening the permanent dimness of Kirin Taq.

"Kettin's inside, rightsome," she replied. "But not to be eyemet. He's asleep."

Asleep, Ty thought. *Good.* His hand, hanging by his side, flicked a sign to the one who was watching, unnoticed by Mila.

"Are you suretain?" Ty asked, effortlessly speaking the curious, hybrid language of the Fallen Sun, with which they recognized each other. Each tribe had a different variation on the language, and whereas tribal colours could be painted on to anyone, learning each tribe's oddities of dialect was an altogether harder matter for impostors to accomplish. "I eyemet him only just, and we arranged to be meeting here."

"True? But he never takes leave without telling me."

"Lessly he parted by the sentry's rung-ladder, nai?" Ty suggested. To prevent the sentries from coming in and out through Kettin's quarters all the time to get to their posts on the first-floor balcony, a rough log ladder leaned against one side. The first-floor wind-holes (there was no glass on Os Dakar) could provide easy access to the balcony.

"Think you?" Mila began, but then caught sight of who was approaching over Ty's shoulder, and relaxed. "Ah! Eyethere. Kettin."

Ty looked around, and saw the twelve-winter, green-haired boy who was Gerdi walking across the torchlit, stony clearing towards him. But then,

Gerdi wasn't trying to make *him* see Kettin in the place of that young boy; only those sentries that observed him, and Mila. His face was set, concentrating. It was a difficult task, to work on manipulating the perception of several people like that, even to one as practised as he was.

He walked up and stood next to Ty. Mila opened the door for him, frowning. "Tribe-captain Kettin. You'd betterly tell me each leavetime."

She was politely berating him for not informing her when he had left his quarters. After all, she had a job to do.

"Be forgivesome," Kettin-Gerdi replied, his voice coming out deep and strong like the older man. Now that he had passed beneath the balcony, and out of the view of the sentries, he could concentrate solely on Mila.

Mila was a little offended by his curt manner, and that she had not been offered an explanation; but she let him by, and Ty with him, assuming that he had had something to drink or was feeling bad. She closed the door behind them, and resumed her post, a little perturbed by the unusual event but convinced that everything was all right now.

Shut away from sight, Ty and Gerdi relaxed for a moment. Smokeless torches burned around them, illuminating a heavy table covered with scraps of food, a few chairs, and a fireplace with no chimney. A set of stone steps led to the wooden upper storeys.

"She'd better be right," Gerdi said quietly. "If he's not asleep, we'll be in a *world* o' trouble."

He didn't really expect an answer, and Ty didn't give him one.

They headed stealthily up the stairs, careful not to make any noise. Gerdi kept up his illusion in case one of the sentries should happen to look in one of the wind-holes as they crossed the first-floor room to the upper sleeping-quarters; but the sentries all had their backs turned, facing outward, and didn't hear a thing. Stepping carefully between the discarded debris that Kettin had left lying around, they softly ascended to the upper level.

There were no wind-holes here, and the torches had been extinguished; but as they poked their heads up through the hatch, the light from below them traced the outlines of the features of the room. A chest, a set of keys, a sleeping-pallet piled with blankets; and hunched under it, the sleeping form of Kettin.

Ty stayed where he was. Quietly, on cat feet, Gerdi crossed the room, treading lightly on the floorboards, until he was standing next to the pallet. Luck was with them; he was lying on his side, his earring-ear up. Gerdi looked at the silver ornament, a thin band speckled with tiny white diamonds. Rubbing his fingers together, he reached for it, to separate the clasp on either side and draw it from the sleeping ear. . .

"That would be wiseless," Kettin spoke, and Gerdi jumped back in alarm. A moment later, he heard the sound of thumping footsteps downstairs, and Ty was pushed roughly up and into the room. A torch was brought, and rested in a wall-sconce. In moments, they were surrounded.

Kettin levered himself up from his bed, looked at them as if they were errant puppies, and sighed wearily. He had a broad face, and a squashed, broken nose, but other than that his bald head and skin colours conformed to the patterns of the tribe. When he spoke, his teeth flashed between his lips, and they were crooked and browned. His eyes were the white of the Kirins, but without his skin colouring or hair visible, it was otherwise impossible to tell him from Dominion-folk. Perhaps, Gerdi realized, that was one reason why they went to so much trouble to paint themselves. Kirins or Dominion-folk; they were all the same here. Hochi might benefit from a little of that philosophy, he mused.

"Bring them withly," Kettin said to his guards, his tone suggesting the depressing predictability of the theft. He was still fully dressed under his blankets, and he walked past them and down the stairs, sparing them not even a glance. The guards, holding them by the arms with the hooked ends of their tribal bola a hair's breath from their napes, manhandled them after him. Nobody spoke.

They were taken to a clearing, a sort of gathering-place that had sprung up in the gap left between two clusters of erratic housing. The ever-present torches burned all around, brightening the endless twilight, and a good portion of the tribe were gathered there, waiting in a wide ring on the stony ground.

By now, Ty had realized that their plan had been anticipated; what he did not expect to see were Kia and the others, standing in the centre of the clearing under the watchful eyes of more tribesmen and women.

Elani watched him appear, brought through the mob towards them. She was holding herself under control, trying to quell the fear that swelled inside her. She had been told of the plan, like the others. But almost as soon as Ty and Gerdi had left, the tribesmen had arrived to grab them. Even Kia and Ryushi couldn't fight all these men and women; after all, the tribespeople had spirit-stones, too. It would be so easy for everyone to gather together, for her to shift, bring them all into the safety of the Dominions and away from Os Dakar. But they didn't have the *earring*, and Kia had gone to great pains to explain how important that was. As if she needed telling.

So she waited, a maturity born of years of hardship keeping her childish panic under a lid.

"They had nothing to—" Ty began to protest to

Kettin as he saw them, but a sharp elbow in the back of his head silenced him brutally.

He and Gerdi were shoved over to join the others, and then the guards retreated to a distance. They stood there for a minute, enduring the gazes of the surrounding mob. Most of them were centred on Ty, the only spot of red-and-blue in an island of strangers; the looks were a blend of hate, suspicion and puzzlement.

Then Kettin stepped up to them, and with him came a familiar figure, accompanied by his huge, loping grey dog. Ty stepped forward to the front of them, to meet his leader. Kia's eyes flickered nervously over his back.

"Whist told me this could happen, nai?" Kettin said, his voice loud enough so they could all hear. "That tribe-brother Ty's friends could regrab him

from us. I disbetrusted him. Not Pilot Ty, I told
him. Nai." He turned his gaze away from Ty,
raking it over the assembled others. Elani quailed,
sniffing back frightened tears, burrowing closer to
Ryushi. "But eyemeet him now, our Pilot. Caught
in the event of attrying to murder me as I slept."

Nobody argued the charge. It was pointless. It
didn't make any difference. Besides, they wouldn't
have been heard over the roar of indignation and
anger that erupted from the mob. Kettin paced
before them, his feet crunching gravel. Behind him,
the eclipsed sun of Kirin Taq presided over them
with disinterest. Suddenly, he leaned in closer to Ty.

"But faithloyal Whist told me something else,
too," he hissed, so only Ty could hear. "Your
friends have a way off Os Dakar, nai?"

Ty looked blandly past him at Whist, the young,

37

lean boy with the crazy multicolour hair. His gaze was returned with an expression that said: *We all do what we gotta do.*

"Now tribe-brother Ty underknows," Kettin said, raising his voice to the mob and swivelling with a magnanimous gesture, "that he is the solely one that can driverate the mashsmashing Bear Claw. And without the Bear Claw, the Fallen Sun cannot continue our goodly work, nai? He under*knows* we cannot murder him as he wouldly murder me." There was a pause, and then a grin spread across his face, displaying his crooked teeth. "But we can murder his friends, nai?"

"Kill them and I'll never drive for you again," Ty growled over the new tumult of approval from the mob, purposely using his usual Dominion-speech instead of the mangled grammar of the Fallen Sun.

"Then we murder them onely by onely," replied Kettin. "Every waketime. Until we murder a friend you care about *realsome*."

His eyes flicked to Kia, then back to Ty, letting him know that he knew. Ty's face tightened.

"Unless we tell you about how we're to get off Os Dakar?" Ty said. The crowd's cries had died now, but their conversation was still only audible to those right next to them. Blink snuffed in the background, then began to worry at an itch in his haunch.

"Unless," Kettin agreed.

"So you can leave, take a few of your closest with you?" Ty asked.

Kettin grinned. "You underestimate me. All the Fallen Sun, Pilot Ty. All the Fallen Sun are my closest. Even faithloyal Whist and his dog."

Whist, who had crouched to pat Blink, looked up at Ty with an odd smile. Ty ignored him, his gaze locked with Kettin's.

"You made me a murderer," he said.

"Murder is a way of life on Os Dakar. I'm attrying to change that."

"But you're willing to run away, to get off this place, if you get the chance."

"You have your friends, I have mine. We leavetake if we can. Betterly for the Fallen Sun."

The crowd were stirring impatiently now, eager to know what Kettin intended to do with the prisoners, craning to hear their private conversation. Ty and Kettin faced each other, almost palpable tension crackling between them. If Ty told Kettin how they intended to get off Os Dakar, they would become expendable. They wouldn't even need the Bear Claw any more. He and his friends would almost certainly be killed for his crime against the Fallen Sun. He knew how these things worked; he'd seen it before.

Matters were complicated by the fact that he didn't *know* how Kia intended to get them off the plateau; she hadn't told him. But it was his one and only lever in this debate, and he had to try and bluff until he could come up with something better.

The crowd finally fell silent, the quiet radiating outwards from where Ty and Kettin locked wills, his dark blue eyes linked with Kettin's cream-on-white. Nothing stirred. Even the wind seemed to die.

And then, faintly, came a noise. At first, it was the tiniest buzz on the edge of their consciousness, a sound without definition and near-unnoticeable.

Then it began to take shape. One by one, the sharpest ears in the crowd turned their heads unconsciously, noting it. A rapid, staccato tapping; many rhythms overlapping into a frenzied jumble. Now they could all hear it, and Kettin broke off from Ty to turn towards its source. But it didn't seem to *have* a source; it was coming from all around them. Louder and louder. Inexorable. Unstoppable.

"*Keriags!*" one of the sentries yelled. "*Thousands* of *Keriags!*"

For a second, everything was frozen. No, it was *impossible*, Kettin thought. There were no Keriags on Os Dakar, except those few that acted as sentries. They were the shock troops of the Princess Aurin, not indigenous scavengers like the Snappers. Why would they be here? They *couldn't* be here.

He turned back to the prisoners with a look of naked hate.

Unless the Keriags had come for *them*.

The second was over, and the stockade burst into pandemonium. The renowned discipline of the Fallen Sun collapsed in a shambles. The crowd scattered in all directions, half of them heading to man the wall defences, half of them fleeing aimlessly in panic. The other tribes on Os Dakar, those they could handle. But there were not more than two hundred in the whole of the Fallen Sun tribe, and each Keriag was worth five men at least. They were many times outnumbered.

The prisoners were forgotten in the sudden rush, and Hochi tried to sweep up Elani protectively in his arms as tribesmen shoved and jostled past them, a blurred sea of red and blue.

But he was too slow; someone fell into her, and she was crushed underneath them. The tribesman scrabbled off her and ran, heedless of what he had done; but when Hochi scooped Elani up, he saw with horror that her black hair was wet with blood, and her eyes were closed. In the same instant, Ty leaped on Kettin, who was glaring in disbelief at the chaos all around him, and bore him to the ground. Kettin fell badly, winding himself; and as he struggled for breath, his Kirin eyes bulging, Ty hooked two fingers around his earring and pulled it roughly from his ear, tearing a bloody path through his lobe. Kettin tried to howl, but his breath was locked in his chest, and he could only gasp as Ty stole the hooking-flail from his belt and ran with his prize, shouting for the others to follow him as he disappeared out of the torchlight.

Somewhere, the Keriags had reached the stockade walls. The Fallen Sun tribe had similar fortifications to those of the Forgotten Legion, with cruel, uneven spikes jutting outwards at angles that supposedly made a direct assault impossible. Not for the Keriags, though. Their six long, spider-like, knob-kneed legs were armoured with a horny black chitin, and they simply sped up the walls, using the jagged edges as footholds. Their bodies, cradled between their legs, weaved around the spikes, their forelimbs clutching their *gaer bolga.* The best defences in Os Dakar were no defence against a Keriag, and they scuttled up and over the fortifications as easily as if they were flat ground. Ty heard the screaming begin as the first of the creatures made its slaughterous path inward.

"Where are we going?" Kia yelled at Ty over the sounds of panic.

"The escape tunnel's over that way!" Gerdi cried, pointing away across the camp.

"Let Kettin take the tunnel. I'll bet my life the Keriags have already found it, somehow," Ty said grimly. "We're going for the Bear Claw."

But he didn't have time to voice the terrible understanding that had suddenly presented itself to him. Why here? Why now, that the Keriags attacked? And then it had all made sense, why Macaan had ordered him kept alive and sent to Os Dakar instead of being executed. Because the King knew that Kia and Ryushi would come for their friend, if they knew he was here; and he had undoubtedly spread the word widely enough so that Parakkan spies could not fail to come across it.

46

The Jachyra had been keeping a watch on him the whole time, waiting for the children of the traitor to turn up so the Keriags could kill them.

"What about El? Is she alright?" Ryushi asked Hochi, who bore her in his massive arms.

"I don't know," he muttered, looking at the unconscious child, cradled against his chest. "I don't know."

They ran onward, ignored by the tribesmen now, just another part of the nightmarish madness that had suddenly swooped on their world. The air was thickening with the sounds of combat and the cries of those who fell before the silent killers that were swarming into the stockade. The shambolic huts and buildings swept past on either side of them, meaningless, leaning in closely as if to hem

47

them up as they dodged from torchlight to shadow, torchlight to shadow.

And then, suddenly, there it was. Nestled between two storage sheds, grey under the faint light of Kirin Taq's sun: the Bear Claw.

It was huge, a towering monstrosity of blackened iron and oil, of pipes and pistons. Rising high above them, it brooded in its own blackness, like a sleeping behemoth waiting to be roused. If it could have been said to have a shape, it would have been vaguely cylindrical; but the innumerable protrusions – spikes, juts, cupolas, bladed fins – rendered any kind of symmetry impossible. It squatted between two enormous caterpillar tracks, humping up on either side like shoulders. It was, like everything else on Os Dakar, a bizarre assemblage of whatever materials and ideas had been at hand at the time. Some things, like the heat-exhaust pipes that bristled along its back, had an obvious purpose. Most things did not, occupying a strange position between protection and ornamentation, and making the whole vast beast seem like a scrappy, but nevertheless fearsome, clutter of junk.

Their moment of awe was destroyed by a terrible, bellowing howl that slit the sky around them, echoing like a thunderclap across Os Dakar. Kia's spine froze, and she was struck by an awful realization. The thing, the creature that had been kept at the bottom of the Snapper Run, the one that had almost bitten her arm off through its gate. Someone had released it. The monster was out.

"Come on!" Ty yelled, urging them onward.

They ran into the shadow of the massive

Machinist vehicle, their feet crunching the loose gravel beneath them, following Ty to where a set of rungs, jutting from the side of the Bear Claw, led up to the wide roof. So intent were they on their destination that they almost did not hear that their footsteps were suddenly being punctuated by a higher, clicking tap, rapidly approaching. But then Tochaa swung around, his terse bark of alarm alerting the others, and they looked back to see a pair of Keriags skitter from behind a dangerously listing two-storey building and fix them with their black eyes.

"Get up there! Go!" Ryushi shouted at Ty, shoving him towards the rungs. "Start it up. We'll hold them off."

Ty hesitated for a moment, his gaze flicking to Kia, who was weaponless like the rest of them;

only he was armed, and Kettin's hooking-flail would be useless to anyone but him. Still, he saw the sense in what Ryushi said, and he wasted no more than an instant on indecision before he threw himself up the rungs and began clambering to the top.

Ryushi glanced back at the child Elani, held in Hochi's arms, a thin ribbon of blood trailing from her hairline. There would be more Keriags here any moment; he could hear the approach of the hordes that clambered over the ineffective defences of the stockade. If she was hurt, hurt badly . . . then there was no chance for them. All their prayers of escape were invested in that little girl, the Resonant. If she didn't recover soon, they could not hope to hold out, even with the formidable powers they wielded between them.

51

"Hochi! Try and wake her!" Kia ordered, sharing Ryushi's thoughts. She had not lost the tone of command that she had acquired over her time in Gar Jenna. If it sounded a little cruel and callous, she couldn't help that now. Their lives were on the line, and perhaps the lives of everyone in the Dominions, if they couldn't get King Macaan's earring to Parakka. She turned back to the approaching danger. "I'll handle these."

The Keriags came towards them, their spindly legs tapping the ground urgently, the jagged sides of their *gaer bolga* catching the torchlight. Kia's head bowed, her eyes closed; and suddenly the stones in her back flared dark red, and the Keriags' onward progress was brutally arrested by an earthen pair of hands, which darted out of the solid ground and gripped on to the hindmost leg of each of them. Surprised, they were not quick enough to avoid being trapped in the crushing grip, but they reacted to their predicament with inhuman speed, instantly turning the edges of their spears to hack at their restraints.

But the ground here was tough and stony, and it did not yield easily under their strikes. Instead, the rest of the golem began to slowly form out of the ground, Kia bringing it up, shaping it, as if it were ascending on a platform out of the solid earth. First the forearms that supported the strong hands; then the chest, with the golem's crude face set deep within it; and then the massive thighs, knees and feet, ending in a thick fringe of roots. Dragging the thrashing Keriags up by their legs, it grew to its full height, lifting them struggling off the ground with ease . . . and then, it raised them up and

53

smashed them to the ground, where they lay crumpled and broken.

Behind her, only vaguely aware of what was going on, Hochi was stroking Elani's hair, shaking her gently. "Come on, girl. Come back. You just took a knock, that's all. You'll be okay." And indeed, the wound on her head was not as bad as it first appeared. It bled a lot, but that was the way of all head wounds, big or little. But it was not deep. Just a gash.

Of course, if she didn't regain consciousness soon, it wouldn't matter how deep it was. None of them would ever leave this plateau.

Hochi tilted his head up, looking out at the shadowy alleys between the buildings that crowded close. The Keriags were getting closer, fast. And this time, the single golem that stood in the Parakkans' defence would not be enough to stop them.

Above them, Ty pulled himself up the last of the rungs, clambering on to the roof of the Bear Claw. The entrance hatch was in front of him, an iron rectangle of riveted metal that provided access to the cockpit of the vehicle. All around him, the protrusions and lumps that crowded the Bear Claw's back confused the eye. He turned around and shouted down to the others: "Come on! Move it!" Waiting long enough to see that some of them, at least, had begun to ascend after him, he turned back to the hatch.

And saw Whist crouched there, three of his sharp-ended discs held between the fingers of his armoured glove, the omnipresent Blink by his side.

"You're not going nowhere without me," he snarled.

"Get out of the way," Ty said, his voice like grit.

"If you're getting off Os Dakar, I'm coming with you," Whist repeated, his painted face deadly serious, his gloved hand hovering, ready to throw its deadly payload.

"After what you've done? I doubt it."

"You know what it's like here. You play the hands you're sure of."

"So now you don't have Kettin to protect you any more," Ty said, mock-sympathetic. "Really, I'd cry blood for you if I had time. But I don't. Get out of my way."

Blink growled, low in his throat.

Tochaa and Gerdi were halfway up the side of the

Bear Claw when the second wave of Keriags arrived, breaking on the shabby buildings and washing down the narrow alleys towards them. Hochi was frantically patting Elani's face, urging her to wake up. Kia's eyes were closed in concentration, her attention focused on the golem that she animated. Ryushi stood next to her, as weaponless as she was, but with his stones boiling full of power. Once he let it go, he wouldn't be able to rein it in again. Not until he had drained himself dry. He would have one chance, and one chance only.

Would it be enough?

The Keriags fell on the golem like a swarm of locusts, presuming it to be the greatest threat. It was a terrifying sight, like razorfish converging on a wounded animal and stripping it to the bone. In seconds, the huge creature was roaring, subsumed under the tide of black, horny chitin, the Keriags easily evading its grasping hands with their superior speed. The shafts of their *gaer bolga* thrust in and out like the pistons of the magma derricks that loomed over Tusami City, stabbing and slashing, their backward-angled serrations tearing out chunks of the golem's earthy flesh as they were pulled free.

But the massacre of the golem only delayed the oncoming assault; for those Keriags that poured up behind the thrashing, bellowing mass merely swept around it, like a wave around a rock, and came skittering down towards the Bear Claw, their black eyes shining under their thick brows of jagged chitin.

Ryushi's fist clenched hard, the veins on the back of his hands standing out.

Then the Flow burst through him, sweeping along his veins like floodwater, blasting out of his outstretched hands to meet the attack, a vast, invisible pulse of concussion that swept forth in an arc. The air warped as the pulse drove it outward, a ripple, a wall of force that bulged around them and then smashed into the Keriags, blasting them apart, scattering them like dust, obliterating everything in its path. The nearest buildings collapsed, blown into rubble and splinters. The beleaguered golem was shattered, suffering the same fate as those who clung to it.

Somewhere, something huge roared, lifting its furious voice to the sky, a savage exultation in its freedom.

Ryushi became aware that he was yelling, the sound gradually sifting into his consciousness in the aftermath of the destruction. His cry died, leaving nothing but silence, a blasted world facing them in the twilight. For fifty feet in front of him, a patch of land had been cleared of everything, stripped clean. Beyond that, there were crumpled buildings, unidentifiable chunks of matter, things he would rather not think about.

But then the skittering started again. For the Keriags were endless, and more were on their way. And Ryushi had not a scrap left in him to protect them. He felt the exhaustion of draining his stones swoop upon him, felt Kia catch him and then stagger herself. She, too, was tired. Not like he was, but tired enough. The next Keriag attack would be the last thing they saw.

He looked back at Hochi. If it had not been for the fact that it was an unpardonable breach of manners to enquire about someone else's spirit-stones, he would have screamed: *Can't you do anything?* at the bigger man. How stupid, that here on the brink of the end he should care about the social niceties of the Dominions. But there it was; it was an irrevocable part of their lives, that if a person chose not to reveal what their powers were, that they should respect that decision. Even unto death.

Behind them, in Hochi's arms, Elani stirred weakly.

Ty didn't know what the awesome burst of force was below them, but he felt the backlash of it across his shoulders. He was thrown forward into Whist, who was similarly surprised; but at the last moment he turned his fall into a dive, tackling his opponent to the bulkhead of the Bear Claw. The metal discs in Whist's hands flew free, rolling crazily away from them. Blink had fallen back, stunned by the eruption; now a flailing boot from Whist caught him on the side of his head, sending him sliding away on his side to thump into a steel heat-exhaust pipe with a whimper of pain.

The torchlight that had surrounded their position had been snuffed out by Ryushi's blast, and now Kia squinted into the unfamiliar pockets of darkness that sprawled among the rubble, trying to catch a sight of their enemy. The skittering of the Keriags had been drowned out now, pushed under by a low thunder that was getting louder, approaching, seeking the source of the destruction that had been felt right across the camp.

Three Keriags appeared, coming from their right, racing towards them suddenly. Kia twisted towards them, still holding her weakened twin. It would do no good. They had no defence. She could muster enough to delay them, maybe, but it would be a momentary grace.

Still, wasn't that one more moment worth trying for?

She never had time to answer her own question, because just then something massive lunged out of the darkness behind the Keriags, gathering them all in a single snap of its wide, fang-stuffed mouth and tossing them away. Kia's pupils dilated to pinpricks and her jaw fell open as she saw, at last, the creature that had been imprisoned in the Snapper Run. She did not know how it had got free. Maybe Kettin had released it, to cover his escape by sowing havoc, attacking friend and foe alike on its rampage.

It didn't matter, she thought, as it raised its head high and loosed a deafening bellow, a great sub-bass boom that rocked them all, these tiny figures that stood terrified in its presence. It didn't matter at all. It was here now, and that was the end of it.

It loomed over them, a massive, leathery thing with a humped back, standing on four huge legs that ended in three-toed claws. In the twilight, it was part of the shadow it had been born from, a huge silhouette against the Kirin Taq sun, of which the only distinct features were the two small, wide-set eyes and the vicious rows of long, narrow teeth, each as long as a man's arm.

Tochaa and Gerdi were paralyzed like the rest

of them, near the top of the rungs on the side of the Bear Claw.

The monster's bellow faded, and in the silence that followed, it swung its blunted head to fix its cold gaze on them.

Ty had lashed a punch into Whist's face, and was drawing back for another one, when he heard the creature below. Like rabbits before a lion's roar, the two combatants looked up, frozen.

Only one of those present did not. Blink.

Ty saw him moving out of the corner of his eye, racing to save his master. He had recovered fast from his blow, scrabbling to his feet and launching himself into a run, fangs bared, paws galloping over the roof of the Bear Claw towards Ty. The sight of the huge dog bearing down on him was

Broken Sky ━━◄━━━━

enough to break Ty's paralysis, and he threw
himself off Whist just as Blink gathered himself,
bunching the muscles of his back legs to pounce.
Ty scrambled away on his back, but he was too
late to do anything about Blink's charge, and the
dog pounced through the air at him, heading for
his exposed throat. Frantically, moving on instinct,
he drew his knees up into his body, the soles of his
boots waiting to bear the brunt of the assault. He
felt the breathtaking weight of the huge dog as his
feet caught it just under the forelegs, and his knees
were slammed back into his chest, bruising the
muscle there; but then he shoved off, throwing the
snarling mass of teeth and sinew away from him.
At the same moment, Whist was getting to his feet,
and Blink slammed into him, taking him off-
balance. He staggered backwards, the dog

66

entangled in his arms, and then pitched backwards and over the edge of the Bear Claw with a cry, disappearing from sight.

Elani screamed in Hochi's arms.

Her eyes had flickered open at the sight of the awesome creature that threatened them. They had focused, unfocused, fixed; and terror had swamped her, naked panic. She scrambled and thrashed in Hochi's arms, for she saw the beast rear at the sound of her shriek, shifting its attention to her, drawing back to bite at them.

Ryushi and Kia realized what was going to happen at the same moment. They threw themselves into Hochi, surrounding him and Elani with their arms, pushing them back against the cold body of the Bear Claw.

The monster lunged forward, teeth blurring in the twilight.

As one, they shut their eyes.

And the jaws snapped shut on nothing, nothing at all, and where there had been a huge machine, there was now an emptiness. The monster paused. For a moment, its tiny mind processed what had happened. Then it turned away, the massive bulk of its head swinging around and towards where the sounds of combat still raged.

There was much prey tonight.

3

More Than a Lifeline

From above, the forest was quiet, a vast, gently rippling blanket of yellow leaves that rested between the cradling arms of the mountains.

Under the skin of foliage, it was a different story.

Gar Jenna resounded to the clanks and thumps of action. Boots pounded the sturdy wooden platforms that jutted from the rock walls, hundreds of feet above the thin ribbon of river at the canyon floor. The walkways that were strung across the chasm were alive with traffic. Everywhere, people were moving, hauling loads or running to and fro. Pulleys whined as they operated lifts, shifting equipment and personnel between the many levels of the village, past the buildings and gantries that clung to the sheer sides of the chasm like limpets. Gar Jenna was mobilizing.

"The troops from Eran Tor have sent word," said the messenger, bowing low as he spoke. "They're ready and waiting."

"Good," Otomo said. The craggy face of the Keeper Elect of Gar Jenna was impassive beneath his grey-white hair, faded with the passing of fifty winters. He stood on the edge of the canyon, surrounded by the yellow-leaved nanka trees and yuki bushes that carpeted the forest-bowl, watching the activity beneath him. Overhead, the artificial leaf canopy that hid Gar Jenna from the air had been drawn across, and the thick ropes and pulleys that held it in place creaked gently in the slight wind.

The messenger looked at him expectantly, waiting to be dismissed; but Otomo suddenly asked: "How many wyverns can they muster?"

"The stables have produced four, perhaps five fighting wyverns," the messenger replied. The stables at Erin Tor had only recently been established, unlike Hochi's stud in Tusami City or Banto's in the mountains. But, of course, the latter two had been seized by Macaan's troops; they had managed to salvage only a few wyverns from potentially dozens, and then only because the creatures had chanced to return to Parakka roosts elsewhere.

"How many does that make in all?" Otomo asked, his broad arms folded across his barrel chest. The messenger looked worried for a moment, and was preparing to politely tell the Keeper that he didn't know, he was just a messenger, when someone else spoke up from behind him.

"Thirty, or forty-five if Amanu Temple makes the muster. But we're short of riders."

Calica walked up to stand next to Otomo. She made a small bow with her head, her orange-gold hair slipping across her cheeks, and then turned to the messenger. "Thank you. Tell Erin Tor we are glad to have them with us, and to wait for the order to assemble."

The messenger bowed low and hurried away, into the surrounding trees. Calica's olive eyes followed Otomo's faded blue ones, watching the people of Gar Jenna swarming around many dozens of metres beneath them.

"They'll need a target," Otomo said.

"We don't have a target to give them," Calica replied.

"We have too *many* targets," he said.

"Which is exactly why we have to choose the right one," Calica answered. "You think we should try and take on Macaan's palace? I don't."

"We can't just wait to see what Macaan does, and then try to stop him. We're too small a force for defence," Otomo said, his voice deep and strong. "The only way we're going to win is if we attack."

"Attack *what*? The palace? Those huge termitary mounds? Maybe we could try and reclaim our posts in Tusami City?" Calica glanced sideways at him. "We'll only get one chance at this. We have to know we're going to do some good."

Otomo's massive shoulders lifted and settled in a sigh. "We should have tried harder. Even with our best spies, we couldn't get close enough. The Jachyra are too cursed good."

Calica was silent. She knew what had become of their people at the hands of Macaan's secret police. It wasn't something she preferred to think about.

"Have you any word on the betrayer?" Otomo said at length.

"We have no idea."

"So now we know little more than we did before," he concluded grimly. "Only that, whatever is going to happen, it's going to happen soon."

"Unless, of course," Otomo's voice continued in Calica's other ear, "that particularly handsome green-haired kid and his friends come up with something in Os Dakar."

Otomo and Calica turned as one to see . . . *Otomo*, standing there with his arms crossed in an exact replica of the way he always stood. Otomo swore in surprise at seeing himself, and Calica's hand flew to her heart, a smile breaking on her face as she realized who it was.

"Gerdi, you *startled* me," she chided.

The other Otomo was gone, and in his place stood the young Noman boy, beaming a cheeky grin at them. "Sorry. Couldn't resist. How's tricks, anyway? What's all this about?" He motioned at the frantic activity below them in the canyon.

"Are you all alright?" Calica asked, her shock

being replaced by relief and excitement that he had made it back from Os Dakar. "Did you get Ty? Is Ryushi okay?"

"Ryushi, eh?" Gerdi insinuated, giving her an exaggeratedly knowing wink.

"Shut *up*," she said, blushing despite herself. Otomo, next to her, tried to suppress a smile. "Are they okay?"

"All present and accounted for," he said. "Course, Elani's a little worse for wear, but then she *did* shift fifty-odd tons of metal as well as seven people across into the Dominions, so you gotta expect that."

"She did what?" Calica asked, not following.

Gerdi grinned. "We got Ty," he said. "And a couple of extra surprises, too. You wanna come see?"

Calica looked at Otomo, half to ask his permission – although she didn't really need it; they were of equal rank, even though she was only seventeen winters and he was three times her age – and half to see if he wanted to come.

"I'll expect a full report tonight at the longhouse," he said, his eyes kindly.

"You'll get it," she said, then ruffled Gerdi's green hair. "I never thought I'd be this happy to *see* you," she announced to the younger boy.

"Touch my hair again and you'll lose that hand," Gerdi said, only half-joking, and then led her off into the forest.

The walk to where the others were took a little less than an hour. On the way, Gerdi recounted to Calica everything that had happened since they had left for Os Dakar, suitably embellishing his own part in the proceedings. It was only fair. After all, since he'd gone to all the trouble of telling the story, he should be allowed to lionize himself a little. Calica repeatedly interrupted him to ask why they had sent Gerdi to come and find her instead of coming themselves, but Gerdi only singsonged "You'll see," and then cackled at the expression of pique on her face.

After a time, the forest petered out and turned into plains at the open end of the mountain range. Out in the clear, the sun of the Dominions was just reaching its zenith, and the faded green grass blew dry under its heat. Calica knew this area; nearby was a cave, where Parakka had often stockpiled supplies and weapons because moving them through the thick forest would be too troublesome. It was empty now; everything had been taken and was being hastily assembled for war.

"Hey!" she heard a shout from the treeline behind them, and she turned to see Ryushi rushing across the grass, a broad smile on his face. She raised her hand in greeting, but to her surprise he swept her up in his arms and hugged her, spinning her around in the air. She returned his hug uncertainly; and when they parted, she looked at him with an odd expression on her face.

"Feeling sprightly today?" she asked sarcastically.

"It's this sunshine," Ryushi replied, blinking up at the blinding orb in the sky. "Didn't realize how much I'd missed it, even for just a few days."

"How're things?" she asked.

"Getting better," he replied. "Kia's almost back to her old self again, since we got Ty. You?"

"Not so good," she admitted. "Macaan's massing his troops. Mostly around his palace, but also around all those weird mounds that I told you about—"

"Ley Warrens," Ryushi interjected.

"So you did find *some*thing out," Calica observed. "Anyway, we're gathering Parakkan forces in secret, but we're far outnumbered. We don't know what Macaan plans to do. We can only wait for him to make his move, and then try and stop him." She glanced at Gerdi, who was wearing a smug grin, and then back at Ryushi. "Unless you two have something to tell me. . .?"

"It's more of a case of what *you* can tell *us*," Gerdi hinted cryptically.

"What's *that* supposed to mean?" she asked, exasperated.

"Come on," Ryushi offered. "I'll show you."

They walked back to where the others were waiting, just inside the edge of the forest, sheltering from the sun. They were sitting around a campfire, above which a small pot of rice and dried fish was simmering, delicious smells wafting from it. Greetings were made all round, and Calica was introduced to Ty. She had to admit, after Ryushi's description of him, she hadn't expected the fierce-looking tribal warrior that stood before her; but when he spoke, he was not half so intimidating as he first appeared and anyway, it took a lot to intimidate Calica. She exchanged nods of mutual respect with Tochaa; they had met before, during Parakka's attempts to set up a branch in Kirin Taq. Elani, who was sitting with her back against a tree, favoured her with a weary smile; but Kia was strangely cold with her, and she saw Ryushi look surprised and disappointed at his sister's reaction. Calica did not share his surprise, however. Kia had been getting gradually more and more hostile towards her ever since they had met. What did Kia have against her, anyway?

"What happened to that Whist guy you were telling me about?" she asked Gerdi.

Gerdi scratched his ear and shrugged. "Everything that was touching the Bear Claw when Elani shifted us got brought over into the Dominions. He and his dog weren't. Ty says they went off the edge, but as to what happened to him . . . I dunno, I'm just glad he's gone."

"The Bear Claw? What?" Calica asked. "Is that the other surprise?"

"Later," Ryushi said. "Sis, you got that earring?"

"Like I'm going to *forget* it," Kia chided him, passing over the small band of silver, studded with miniscule diamonds. Her eyes flicked to Calica for an instant, and she seemed to freeze over a little; but the moment passed, and all was normal again.

"This," said Ryushi, "is King Macaan's own earring."

"Hopefully," Ty added, reminding them all that they only had Kettin's word it was genuine. But Calica didn't seem to hear; her attention was fixed entirely on the object held out in Ryushi's hand.

"Really?" she asked, her face transformed by wonder. "Is it really?"

Ryushi glanced sidelong at Ty. "Well, we were kinda hoping you could tell us."

"Give it to me," she said, and as Ryushi delivered it into her hand, she wore an expression of complete hope and fascination. If this was what he said it was, then this was more than a lifeline for Parakka; this could be the key to the whole of Macaan's plan.

The earring, dropped from Ryushi's hand, seemed to fall in slow motion towards her cupped palms, like a stone dropped in honey.

It touched her skin, and she was buried under the explosion of visions that hit her, smashing into her, sending her spinning into blackness. . .

. . .and then she was *behind* his eyes, riding in the head of the young prince, but she couldn't see very much because of the tears that blurred everything and made the torchlight sparkle. What she did see was a death-bed, and on it two people, a man and a woman. Father and Mother. His father was a Kirin, his mother fair and blonde, a Dominion woman. But both of them had been ravaged by the terrible disease that had carried them off, and the boy was yet young, so young. He turned his head, and Calica travelled with him, to lay his eyes on a young Dominion girl, one of his mother's serving-maids, and Calica knew with a foresight that was not hers that he would marry this girl one day, and that she would bear him a daughter, and then be taken from him by the same disease that had laid his parents to rest. . .

. . .and now he was a King, the ruler of Kirin Taq,

who had built on his father's legacy to subjugate all opposition against him. Calica watched as the last of the thanes of Kirin Taq knelt before him. And all around were the black-armoured forms of the King's Guardsmen, the troops that had been his father's and were now his. He turned away from the defeated thane, Calica travelling with him, and walked through the cool corridors of the palace towards his daughter's bedchamber. His wife was already dead by now, and Calica felt the pain as keenly as if it were her own. How strange, that a monster like this could love so deeply. But then he was leaning over his baby daughter, sleeping in her crib, and waving away the Guardsmen who watched over her. The door swung shut behind him with a heavy thump.

"All this for you," he said, and in those words

Calica felt the deep adoration he had for his daughter, the only part of his wife he had left; and she knew, with a sharp twist of sorrow, that as his daughter grew she would not reciprocate that love, but be cold and cruel and beautiful. . .

. . .and now Calica saw her, as a young woman, tall and slender and proud, with raven-black hair plaited in twists and falling over a simple blue gown. And she recognized those sculpted cheekbones, those ice-blue eyes, the perfect mouth twisted in a triumphant smile. Aurin. The Princess Aurin, ruler of Kirin Taq; for that was what she was, now. But there was something curious in the sight, something fundamentally disturbing, because her recognition of the Princess was not just through the King's eyes, but through her own as well. For though she had never physically laid eyes on Aurin, there was . . . *something* . . .

. . .and now Calica felt Macaan's pride as he left his daughter to rule over the subjugated land, while he massed his army around him and made ready to leave for new territories. For his desire to conquer was insatiable; she felt Macaan's thoughts writhing in his brain, telling him that his days were numbered, that one day the disease that had taken his parents and lover away from him would be back, and this time it would be *him* it claimed. The King was working against time, trying to obtain the world for his daughter and knowing, deep down, that even that would not be enough to wring love from her heart. . .

. . .and now Macaan is King of the Dominions, too. His army of Guardsmen have taken the old King by surprise, appearing on the battlefield as if from nowhere and annihilating the pitiful inland defence, cutting off supplies to the coast and then sweeping out to finish the job. Because Macaan has a machine, a machine powered by Resonants, with a strength so great that it can shift whole armies across the time-gap between Kirin Taq and the Dominions. But there is a problem; it can be used only once, for the Resonants are frail things and don't survive the transition. That one time is enough to crush King Oko and his Knights, and take over the Dominions. But it is not enough to fulfil him. Even now, he isn't satisfied with what he has; because he lacks the forces to achieve complete control, and only complete control will secure his daughter's reign. So he turns his mind to the plan. . .

"*Oh!*" Calica yelped, dropping the earring as if it had burned her. For a moment, she looked like a frightened animal, paralyzed by a predator; but then her eyes calmed a little, and she looked around the faces that peered at her in concern.

"Are you okay?" Ryushi asked. "You can't have held it for more than a second."

"The plan! The *plan!*" Calica cried, springing to her feet. "I know what he's going to do!"

What *is* Macaan's dastardly plan, and will it
be easily thwarted?

There's only one way to find out. . .

Broken Sky

ACT 1 PART 9
coming soon

GET YOUR
Broken Sky
BOOKS HERE!

Is your collection of BROKEN SKY incomplete? Are you missing some vital instalments? Well. . .

If you're having trouble finding copies, write to us with a cheque or postal order made payable to Scholastic Ltd at the following address:

Scholastic Ltd
Westfield Road
Southam
Warwickshire CV33 0JH

and we'll send you the books you're after. Remember to give us your name and address, and state clearly which books you want. Each part is £1.99 and there's a new one out each month to collect and cherish!

REMEMBER – THE SERIAL CONTINUES.
DON'T FIGHT IT.